What Shall We Do With The Boo-hoo Baby?

For perplexed parents everywhere — C.C.

ISBN 0-439-33724-0

12 11 10 9 8 7 6 5 4 3 2 1   1 2 3 4 5 6/0

Printed in the U.S.A.   14

First Scholastic paperback printing, November 2001

Original book design by Mike Brown.

What Shall We Do With The Boo-hoo Baby?

BY Cressida Cowell ILLUSTRATED BY Ingrid Godon

SCHOLASTIC INC.
New York Toronto London Auckland Sydney
Mexico City New Delhi Hong Kong Buenos Aires

The baby said,

"BOO-HOO-HOO!"

What shall we do with the Boo-hoo Baby?

"Feed him," said the dog.

"BOO-HOO-HOO!"

said the baby.

What shall we do with the
Boo-hoo Baby?

"Bathe him,"
said the cat.

So they gave the baby a bath.

"Bow-wow!"
said the dog.

"Meow!"
said the cat.

"BOO-HOO-HOO!"

said the baby.

What shall we do with the Boo-hoo Baby?

"Play with him," said the cow.

So they played with the baby.

"Bow-wow!"
said the dog.

"Quack!"
said the duck.

"BOO-HOO-HOO!"

said the baby.

What shall we do with the
Boo-hoo Baby?

"Put him to bed,"
said the duck.

So they put him to bed.

"Moo," said the cow.

"Bow-wow," said the dog.

"Meow," said the cat.

"Quack," said the duck,

and . . .

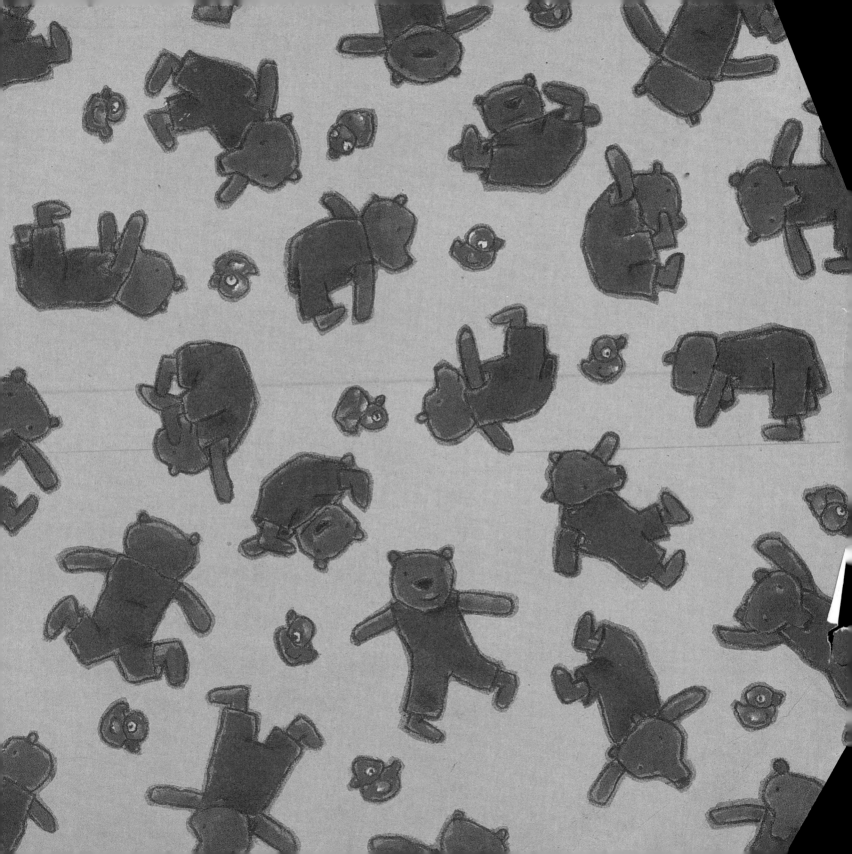